What's in Fox's Sack?

For Annie,
Bob, and Joe

Clarion Books
a Houghton Mifflin Company imprint
215 Park Avenue South, New York, NY 10003
Copyright © 1982 by Paul Galdone
All rights reserved.
For information about permission to reproduce selections from
this book, write to Permissions, Houghton Mifflin Company,
215 Park Avenue South, New York, NY 10003.
Library of Congress Catalog Card Number: 81-10251 ISBN: 0-89919-062-6.
Printed in the USA
WOZ 10 9 8 7

What's in Fox's Sack?

An Old English Tale Retold and Illustrated by

PAUL GALDONE

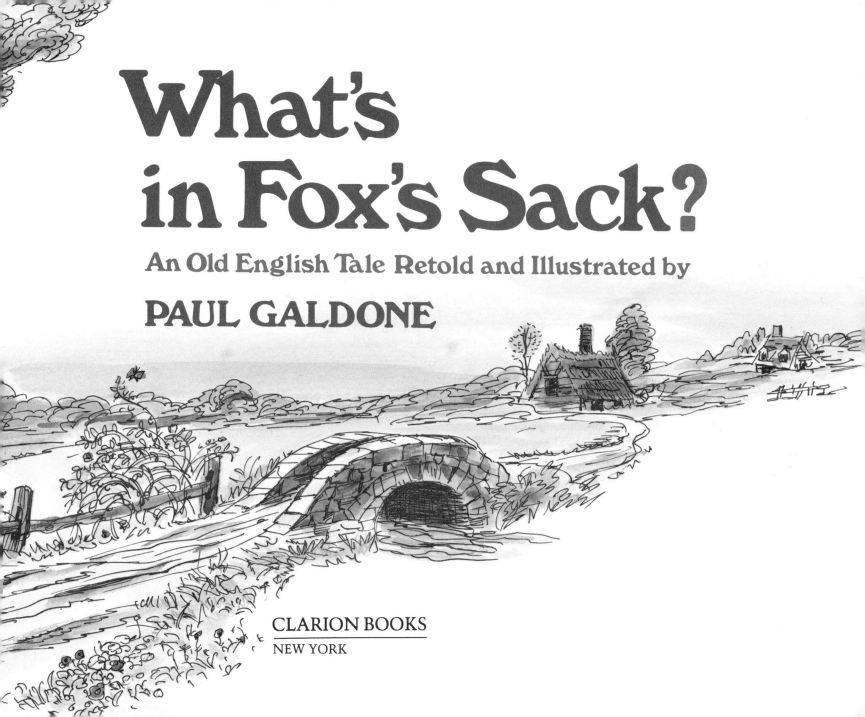

CLARION BOOKS

NEW YORK

ne day Fox was digging by his tree stump when he found a big fat bumblebee. So he put it in his sack.

Then he walked, and he walked, and he walked, till he came to a house.

In the house there was a very little woman sweeping the floor.

"Good morning," said Fox.

"Good morning," said the very little woman.

"May I leave my sack here?" asked Fox.
"I want to go to my friend Squintum's house."
"Yes, certainly," the very little woman replied.
"Very well, then," said Fox. "But mind you don't
look in the sack!"
"Oh, I won't," said the very little woman.

So off went Fox,
trot,trot,
trot-trot-trot,
to Squintum's house.

As soon as he was gone, the very little woman *did* look in the sack.
She just peeped in, and out flew the big fat bumblebee!

And the very little woman's rooster ran and gobbled him up.

Presently, back came Fox. He looked in his sack
and he said, "Where is my big fat bumblebee?"

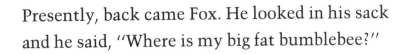

And the very little woman said, "I'm very sorry,
but I'm afraid I *did* look in your sack, and the big fat
bumblebee flew out, and my rooster gobbled him up."

"Oh, really?" said Fox. "Then I shall take your rooster instead."

So he caught the very little woman's rooster and put him in the sack.
Then off he went.

He walked, and he walked, and he walked, till he came to another house.

In this house there was
a very big woman darning socks.

"Good morning," said Fox.

"Good morning," said the very big woman.

"May I leave my sack here while I go to
my friend Squintum's house?" Fox asked.

"Yes, certainly," the very big woman replied.

"Very well, then," said Fox. "But mind you
don't look in the sack!"

"Oh, I won't," said the very big woman.

So off went Fox,
trot, trot,
trot-trot-trot,
to Squintum's house.

As soon as he was gone,
the very big woman
did look in the sack.
She just peeped in,

and out flew the rooster.

And the very big woman's pig chased him down the lane.

Presently, back came Fox.
He looked in his sack and he said,
"Oho! Where is my rooster?"
And the very big woman said,
"I'm very sorry, but I *did* open your sack.
And your rooster flew out,
and my pig chased him down the lane."

"Very well," said Fox. "I shall take your pig instead."
So he caught the very big woman's pig and put him
in the sack. Then off he went.

He walked, and he walked, and he walked, till he came to another house.

In this house there was
a very skinny woman washing the dishes.

"Good morning," said Fox.
"Good morning," said the very skinny woman.
"May I leave my sack here while I go to
   my friend Squintum's house?" Fox asked.
"Yes, certainly," the very skinny woman replied.
"Very well, then," said Fox. "But mind you
   don't look in the sack!"
"Oh, I won't," said the very skinny woman.

So off went Fox,
trot, trot,
trot-trot-trot,
to Squintum's house.

As soon as he was gone, the very skinny woman *did* look in the sack. She just peeped in, and out jumped the pig.

And the very skinny woman's little boy took a stick
and chased him out of the house.

Presently, back came Fox. He looked in
his sack and he said, "Where is my pig?"
And the very skinny woman said, "I'm very
sorry, but I'm afraid I *did* look in your sack.
And the pig jumped out, and my little boy
took a stick and chased him out of the house."

"My goodness," said Fox. "Then I shall have to take your little boy instead." And he took the very skinny woman's little boy and put him in the sack. Then off he went.

He walked, and he walked, and he walked, till he came to another house.

And in this house there was a
very fat woman making gingerbread.
At one side of her sat
three little girls.
And on the other side sat
a big watchdog.

"Good morning," said Fox.

"Good morning," said the very fat woman.

"May I leave my sack here while I go to
   my friend Squintum's house?" Fox asked.

"Yes, certainly," the very fat woman replied.

"Very well, then," said Fox. "But mind you
   don't look in the sack!"

"Oh, I won't," said the very fat woman.

Then off went Fox,
trot, trot,
trot-trot-trot,
to Squintum's house.

Now as soon as he was gone, the lovely smell
of the gingerbread came out of the oven.
It smelled so good that all the three little girls called out,
"Oh, Mother, Mother, may we have some gingerbread?"

And the little boy in the sack called out,
"Oh, may I have some gingerbread, too?"

Well, of course, as soon as the very fat woman
heard a little boy calling from the sack,
she undid it at once. And out climbed the little boy.

And so that Fox
wouldn't notice anything,
the very fat woman
put the big watchdog
in the sack instead.

Presently, back came Fox. He looked at the sack,
and it still looked as full as before. So he picked
it up and off he went.
He walked, and he walked, and he walked,
till he came to a forest. There he stopped to rest.
He put down the sack and said, "It is almost dinnertime.
That little boy will make a very good meal for me!"

And he untied the sack.

Out jumped NOT the little boy, but the BIG WATCHDOG.
Fox was so frightened that he ran away as fast as he could.

When the big watchdog got back home,
the very fat woman was just taking
the gingerbread out of the oven.

She gave pieces to the three little girls
and the little boy. And she gave an
especially BIG piece to the watchdog.